Buy Me Or Fuck Off.

THE
QUEEN

RAT

LOVE HAS NO
BOUNDARIES

Praise for the Book

"...Great Fun..."

-

Professor Stephen Hawking, CH CBE FRS FRSA

"Concise, Rousing and Frequently Moving"

-

The Telegraph

"Greatness"

-

William Shakespeare

"Good"

-

Madonna

"Creative"

-

Dr. Martin Luther King Jr.

AMPUTEE ELF GIVEN TWIG HANDS

SNOWMAN WITH A PENGUIN'S HEAD

First (and probably only) Edition 2018

ISBN-13:
978-1727790191

ISBN-10:
1727790197

The Demented Advent Calendar

G.J. Paterson

To Leeroy,

I hope it's benign!

All my Love,

G. J. Paterson

This Book Belongs To:

....

Who Is Hereby Legally Certified As
NOT A Sex Offender.

This Document May Be Used As Evidence In
A Court Of Law.

December
1st

DONKEY WHO SAW
CHRIST

The Grating

It happened on Valentine's Day. I had everything ready for my big night in with Zandra. I had prepared our romantic meal while she was working late at the sperm bank.

She was what they referred to in the industry as a "milker". She helped the lads make sure that they shot their goo for the sake of medical progress. It wasn't an official title. It wasn't even a real job. But it was her life.

And whether I liked it or not it put bread on the table. The bread in question was made from the hardened crust of what Zandra called "jizzum run-off". I hated the taste of this bread but she demanded that I eat it.

I was so looking forward to having a proper meal tonight. It wouldn't just be a treat for Zandra, but for me as well. I hadn't eaten dinner without jizzum run-off bread for nearly two years now. I could not wait for some proper food.

Who knows, maybe Zandra would even treat me to a handy of my own. She hadn't pleasured me in months. She said that she was over fatigued from the hours of giving intimate massages at work. Therefore she had lost all interest in it when she came home.

The dinner smelled delicious. As the aroma hit my nostrils I suddenly became very hungry. I couldn't help myself. I just had to open up the oven and eat some of the goose before it was ready. I peeled off a piece of its succulent skin and put it to my mouth.

It was only when I had finished consuming the meat that I realized I had burnt my hand quite badly. The skin had collapsed in on itself and the flesh was exposed and sizzling. I was reminded of the goose flesh I had just eaten and cackled.

"HAHAHAHAHAHAHAHAHAHAHAHAHAHAH AHA!"

After ten minutes of laughing to myself I remembered that I had to get the rest of the meal finished before Zandra came home. I swiftly began mixing the salad. Everything was in place. All I had to do was grate some strong cheese on top and I would be finished.

As I began grating I noticed that my hand burn was itching intensely. I tried scratching it but this was ineffective. The itch was deep down, almost to the bone. Then an idea came - I would use the grater!

I began swiftly rubbing the jagged metal instrument against my open wound. The sensation was both soothing and deep, akin to having a feather inserted into one's anus.

I remembered I had an abundance of goose feathers and would make a mental note not to throw them out. I increased the speed with which I was grating. Unbeknownst to me my skin and flesh scrapings were getting all over the salad.

This would not be a problem for me, however. As it turns out, I would never get to see Zandra eat the tainted vegetable and lettuce medley. As I grated faster and faster my hand disappeared. Then my arm, then my leg, then my other arm, then my other leg.

I grated my entire body until I was nothing but meat dust. "This is bloody typical!" I thought to myself as I lay there in the salad bowl.
"How am I going to explain this?"

December 2nd

Jesuses GRADUATION

Everything Must Rhyme! (Or It's Brown Slush Time)

Everything must rhyme in my life, otherwise I get diarrhea.

I'm not good with poetry and big words like onomatopoeia.

My sentences don't need to be lyrical or contain consistent syllables.

They just need to rhyme or I'll shit myself, all over the place - on the kitchen, on the shelf.

It's because I was born wrong, my mother drank bleach while I was in the womb.

She made infant me wear a tight thong and watch Peter Cushing in The Mummy's Tomb.

This caused me great distress, PTSD and an abnormal digestive structure.

Nothing has worked to cure me, not hypnotism, surgery or acupuncture.

So everything I say or write must rhyme in some way, or else my trousers go liquid brown with stinky bum hole clay.

I wish I could get rid of this curse but I continue to suffer in torment.

Every now and then I slip up and must clean the big messes I make.

On occasion I have tried to fight it but this is always a mistake.

Anyway, enough about that. Let's discuss what I want for Christmas this year.

I want to not shit myself anymore when I don't rhyme and to enjoy a tasty beer.

This will never happen though, the hops interfere with my guts.

Doesn't matter if it's craft, lager or ale. It's worse for my stomach than nuts.

(I'm allergic to nuts you see. So can't eat those either. Which is also really annoying.)

Hey, wait a minute, that didn't rhyme and I didn't get the squirts!

My belly didn't gurgle and my rectum didn't hurt.

Let's try this again. I will not rhyme...

AAAAAAAAAAAAAHHHHHHHHH! My anus. That didn't work at all.

I can't believe I had the gall (to try that out.)

Hey, wait a minute, could that be it? Can I say what I want as long as it's in bracket(s)?

(Test. Please don't make me shit my pants.)

Success! Yes!

(Now all I have to do is remember to write in this format then I'll be home free. All I can say is YIPEE!)

AAAAAAAAAAAAAAAAAAAAAAAAAHHHH HH! It happened again! I made brown rain!

Why? I followed the rules. Wait, am I not allowed to rhyme in brackets?

AAAAAAAAAAAAAAAAAHHHHHH! Forgot to rhyme... that... time.

(This is getting hard. So I can't rhyme in these brackets, right?)

But if I rhyme from brackets and back will I still shoot watery shite?

...No...That's interesting...Hello.

I hate my life. Also I just realized Peter Cushing was never in The Mummy's Tomb. I'm just gonna accept my fate and be a walking Nutella hose.

December 3rd

STAR OF
WUNDA
D
STAR OF
LIGHT

Things I Have Used To Replace My Head
Which Have Proven To Be Poor Substitutes

By The Headless Horseman

Pumpkins
Other People's Heads
Cabbages
Swans
A Table Leg
A Chair Leg
A Football
An *American* Football
Plants Of All Shapes And Sizes
Cats
Dogs
Froggs
Bogs
A Big Rocket
Toe Nails
Those Boots You Find In The Sea
Alpaca Fur
The Sabre Tooth From A Sabre Tooth Tiger
Fire
Ice
Rice
An Erotic Calendar
An Erratic Colander

Herbs De Provence
Every Conceivable Part Of A Shovel
An Echo
Fjord Juice
A Black Hole
A White Star
A Red Dwarf DVD Boxset
Pictures Of Your Gran
Whole Grain Bread (Soggy)
Connect Four
A To Scale Replica Of Chucky From Child's Play 3 When He Has Half His Face Sliced Off
Minty Things
Flannels
Wine Gums
A Magnifying Glass

December 4th

OUR BABY JEESUS

A Christmas Carol By Charles Dickens
Part 1

I have changed some of the names and words to ruder ones in order to appeal to a more modern audience. I have also removed some of the longer paragraphs because no one wants a story that is too wordy. I also added more ducks to the story.

Marley was dead, to begin with. There is no doubt whatever about that. The register of his burial was signed by the clergyman, the clerk, the undertaker, and the man who is actually a knee. Boner signed it. And Boner's name was good upon anything he chose to put his hand to. Old Marley was as dead as a succulent duck l'orange.

Boner knew he was dead? Of course he did. Boner never painted out Old Marley's name. There it stood, years afterwards, above the warehouse door: Boner and Marley. The firm was known as Boner and Marley. Some Vaginas people new to the business called Boner Boner, and some Vaginas Marley, but he answered to both names. It was all the same to him.

Oh! but he was a tight-fisted hand at the grindstone, Boner! a squeezing, wrenching, grasping, scraping, clutching, covetous old sinner!

Hard and sharp as a duck, from which no steel had ever struck out generous snorkels; secret, and self-contained, and solitary as a duck with severe depression.

He carried his own low temperature always about with him; he iced his office in the dog-days, and didn't thaw it one degree, even at the festive time of Fart Cannon.

External heat and cold had little influence on Boner. No warmth could warm, no wintry weather chill him. The heaviest rain, and snow, and hail, and sleet could boast of the advantage over him in only one respect. They often 'came down' handsomely, and Boner never did.

Nobody ever stopped him in the street to say, with gladsome looks, 'My dear Boner, how are you? When will you come to see me?' No beggars implored him to bestow a trifle, no children asked him what it was o'clock, no man or woman ever once in all his life enquired the way to such and such a place, of Boner.

But what did Boner care? It was the very thing he liked. To edge his way along the crowded paths of life, warning all human sympathy to keep its distance, was what the knowing ones call 'nuts' to Boner.

Once upon a Vagina — of all the good days in the year, on Fart Cannon Eve — old Boner sat busy in his counting-house. It was cold, bleak, biting weather; foggy withal; and he could hear the ducks in the court outside go wheezing up and down, beating their hands upon their succulent duck breasts, and stamping their duck feet upon the pavement stones to warm them.

The door of Boner's counting-house was open, that he might keep his eye upon his clerk, who in a dismal little cell beyond, a sort of tank, was copying letters. Boner had a very small snorkel, but the clerk's snorkel was so very much smaller. But he couldn't replenish it, for Boner kept the snorkel repair kit in his own room.

'A merry Fart Cannon, uncle! God save you!' cried a cheerful voice. It was the voice of Boner's nephew, who came upon him so quickly that this was the first invagination he had of his approach.

'Bah!' said Boner. 'Humbug!'

He had so heated himself with rapid walking in the fog and frost, this nephew of Boner's, that he was all in a glow; his face was ruddy and handsome; his eyes sparkled, and his breath smelled like your mum.

'Fart Cannon a humbug, uncle!' said Boner's nephew. 'You don't mean that, I am sure?'

'I do,' said Boner. 'Merry Fart Cannon! What right have you to be merry? What reason have you to be merry? You're refrigerator friendly enough.'

'Come, then,' returned the nephew in the style of a homosexual. 'What right have you to be dismal? What reason have you to be morose? You're rich enough.'

Boner, having no better answer ready on the spur of the moment, said, 'Bah!' again; and followed it up with 'Humbug!'

'Don't be cross, uncle!' said the nephew.

'What else can I be,' returned the uncle, 'when I live in such a world of fools as this? Merry Fart Cannon! Out upon merry Fart Cannon! What's Fart Cannon Vagina to you but a Vagina for paying bills without money; a Vagina for finding yourself a year older, and not an hour richer; a Vagina for balancing your books, and having every item in 'em through a round dozen of months presented dead against you? If I could work my will,' said Boner indignantly, 'every idiot who goes about with "Merry Fart Cannon" on his lips should be boiled with his own pudding, and buried with a stake of holly through his heart. He should!'

'Uncle!' pleaded the nephew.

'Nephew!' returned the uncle sternly, 'keep Fart Cannon in your own way, and let me keep it in mine.'

'Keep it!' repeated Boner's nephew. 'But you don't keep it.'

'Let me leave it alone, then,' said Boner. 'Much good may it do you! Much good it has ever done you!'

'There are many things from which I might have derived good, by which I have not profited, I dare say,' returned the nephew; 'Fart Cannon among the rest. But I am sure I have always thought of Fart Cannon Vagina, when it has come round — apart from the veneration due to its sacred name and origin, if anything belonging to it can be apart from that — as a good Vagina; a kind, forgiving, charitable, pleasant Vagina; the only Vagina I know of, in the long calendar of the year, when men and women seem by one consent to open their shut-up hearts freely, and to think of people below them as if they really were fellow-passengers to the grave, and not another race of creatures bound on other journeys. And therefore, uncle, though it has never put a scrap of duck meat in my pocket, I believe that it *has* done me good and *will* do me good; and I say, God bless it!'

The clerk in the tank involuntarily applauded. Becoming immediately sensible of the impropriety, he poked the snorkel, and went back to his rock pooling.

'Let me hear another sound from *you*,' said Boner, 'and you'll keep your Fart Cannon by losing your situation! You're quite a powerful speaker, sir,' he added, turning to his nephew. 'I wonder you don't go into Parliament.'

'Don't be angry, uncle. Come! Dine with us tomorrow.'

Boner said that he would see him — Yes, indeed he did. He went the whole length of the expression, and said that he would see him in that extremity first.

'But why?' cried Boner's nephew. 'Why?'

'Why did you get married?' said Boner.

'Because I fell in love.'

'To a duck?!' growled Boner, as if that were the only one thing in the world more ridiculous than a merry Fart Cannon. 'Good-afternoon!'

'Nay, uncle, but you never came to see me before that happened. Why give it as a reason for not coming now?

'Good-afternoon,' said Boner.

'I want nothing from you; I ask nothing of you; why cannot we be friends?'

'Good-afternoon!' said Boner.

'I am sorry, with all my heart, to find you so resolute. We have never had any quarrel to which I have been a party. But I have made the trial in homage to Fart Cannon, and I'll keep my Fart Cannon humour to the last. So A Merry Fart Cannon, uncle!'

'Good-afternoon,' said Boner.

'And a Happy New Year!'

'Good-afternoon!' said Boner.

His nephew left the room without an angry word, notwithstanding. He stopped at the outer door to bestow the greetings of the season on the clerk, who, cold as he was, was warmer than Boner; for he returned them cordially.

'There's another fellow,' muttered Boner, who overheard him: 'my clerk, with fifteen shillings a week, and a wife and family, talking about a merry Fart Cannon. I'll retire to Bedlam.'

Boner resumed his labours with an improved opinion of himself, and in a more facetious temper than was usual with him. Then he played with his own ejaculate.

(To Be Continued)

December 5th

Why I Blacked Up, Officer

Listen Officer, you've got to believe me. I'm not in black makeup because I'm racist. Far from it! My best friend just got back from Majorca and he is VERY dark now.

Please don't write me a ticket for being a racist man. I can promise you that I am not! I don't want to have to go all the way to court to prove it.

Please, this will get on the news and my kids will leave me and take my wife with them. This will RUIN me! I haven't done anything wrong.

Oh, you want an explanation, huh? That's bloody typical. Don't you have anything better to do? There's a boy there with a plush pink dolphin. WHERE DID HE GET IT FROM? You don't care about the important issues do you?

Don't point that taser at me! I'm a respected member of this community. ...No I am not threatening you! Fuck off, I will kill you if you talk to me like that again!

I'm sorry for being so tense. It's just I REALLY fancy eating some fried chicken. And this isn't me trying to promote a racist stereotype. I am VERY hungry and fried chicken is DELICIOUS.

Fine, I get the message. The sooner I explain why I'm in black face, wearing an afro wig and a "Def 2 Crips" t shirt the sooner I can go home. Well alright then.

The truth is... I AM actually black, Ha! Didn't expect that did you? I can't be racist because this is my own race. So please let me go.

What's that? Why is the black paint on my face running?

I find that to be a very racist question. I have quite the mind to bust a cap in your white ass. Just kidding officer. I'm not violent. I'm just really hungry for that chicken which I have waiting for me at home.

I know I'm sweating. I'm very tense and hungry. Yes I know it looks like my black paint is running and that I have white skin underneath. It's a medical condition.

You know what? YOU'RE the racist for suggesting that if I was white then I'd somehow be different inside than a black man. I think you should let me go before I sue you.

Yes, I'm aware it's illegal to wear an insensitive and racist costume. Yes I know I'm wearing a badge that says "First Prize Racist Fancy Dress Competition."

I found that badge on the side of the road. The sharp pin of it was up in the air. If I had left it then a hedgehog could have had its foot pierced. Poor thing. Do you hate hedgehogs?

You know what? Kiss my black ass. I don't need this. So what if I'm in blackface? At least I'm not a ghost like you. You were a ghost this whole time.

...And so was I.

December 6th

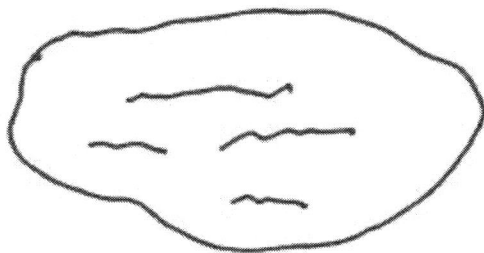

XMAS
PUDDLE :)

A Christmas Carol By Charles Dickens
Part 2

The office was closed in a twinkling, and the duck, with the long ends of his white comforter dangling below his waist (for he boasted no greatcoat), went down a slide on Cornhill, at the end of a lane of boys, twenty Vaginas, in honour of its being Fart Cannon Eve, and then ran home to Camden Town as hard as he could pelt, to play at blindman's- buff.

Then he had a bath.

Now, it is a fact that there was nothing at all particular about the tits on the door, except that they were very large. It is also a fact that Boner had seen them, night and morning, during his whole residence in that place.

And then let any man explain to me, if he can, how it happened that Boner, having his key in the lock of the door, saw in the tits, without its undergoing any intermediate process of change — not tits, but Marley's face.

Marley's face. It was not in impenetrable shadow, as the other objects in the yard were, but had a dismal light about it, like a bad lobster in a dark cellar (Dicken's words, not mine.)

It was not angry or ferocious, but looked at Boner as Marley used to look; with molesterly spectacles turned up on its molesterly forehead. As Boner looked fixedly at this phenomenon, it was tits again.

To say that he was not startled, or that his blood was not conscious of a terrible sensation to which it had been a stranger from infancy, would be untrue. But he put his hand upon the key he had relinquished, turned it sturdily, walked in, and lighted his candle.

Nobody under the table, nobody under the sofa; a small snorkel in the grate; spoon and basin ready; and the little saucepan of gruel (Boner had a cold in his head) upon the hob. Nobody under the bed; nobody in the closet (except Ed); nobody in his dressing-gown, which was hanging up in a suspicious attitude against the wall. Lumber-room as usual. Old snorkel, old shoes, two fish baskets, washing-stand on three legs, and three ducks asleep upon the bed.

Quite satisfied, he closed his door, and locked himself in; double locked himself in, which was not his custom. Thus secured against surprise, he took off his iron crotch guard, put on his steel crotch guard, and sat down before the snorkle to take his gruel.

There was a duck.

'Humbug!' said Boner; and walked across the room.

There were now two ducks.

'It's humbug still!' said Boner. 'I won't believe it.'

His colour changed, though, when, without a pause, it came on through the heavy door and passed into the room before his eyes. Upon its coming in, the dying flame leaped up, as though it cried, 'I know him! Marley's Molester!' and fell again.

...Three ducks.

Boner had often heard it said that Marley had no bowels, but he had never believed it until now.

Twenty. Five. Ducks.

'How now!' said Boner, caustic and cold as ever. 'What do you want with me?'

'Much!' Marley's voice; no doubt about it.

'Who are you?'

'Ask me who I *was*.'

'Who *were* you, then?' said Boner, raising his voice. 'You're particular, for a shade.'

He was going to say 'for a spade', but realised this could be misconstrued as racist.

'In life I was your partner, Ziggy Marley.'

'Can you — can you sit down?' asked Boner.

'I can.'

'Do it, then.'

Only then did he see the wheelchair. Boner asked the question, because he didn't know whether a molester so transparent might find himself in a condition to take a chair; and felt that in the event of its being impossible, it might involve the necessity of an embarrassing explanation. But the Molester managed to find a space not occupied by ducks and sat down.

'You don't believe in me,' observed the Molester.

'I don't,' said Boner.

'What evidence would you have of my reality beyond that of your own senses?'

'I don't know,' said Boner.

'Why do you doubt your senses?'

'Because,' said Boner, 'a little thing affects them. A slight disorder of the stomach makes them cheats. You may be an undigested bit of beef, a blot of mustard, a crumb of cheese, a fragment of an underdone potato.'

'INDEED I AM A POTATO!' countered Marley.

'Oh yes,' thought Boner. He had in fact been a potato this whole time.

The Molester/Potato sat perfectly motionless, its hair, and crisp jacket were still agitated as by the hot vapour from an oven.

'You see this toothpick?' said Boner, returning quickly to the charge, for the reason just assigned; and wishing, though it were only for a second, to divert the vision's stony gaze from himself.

'I do,' replied the Molester.

'You are not looking at it,' said Boner.

'But I see it,' said the Molester, 'notwithstanding.'

'Well!' returned Boner, 'I have but to swallow this, and be for the rest of my days persecuted by a legion of goblins, all of my own creation. Humbug, I tell you: humbug!'

At this the foreskin raised a frightful cry, and shook its chain with such a dismal and appalling noise, that Boner held on tight to his chair, to save himself from falling in a swoon. But how much greater was his horror when the Potato, taking off the bandage round his head, as if it were too warm to wear indoors, its lower jaw dropped down upon its breast!

Boner fell upon his knees, and clasped his hands before his face.

'Mercy!' he said. 'Dreadful apparition, why do you trouble me?'

'Man of the worldly mind!' replied the Molester, 'do you believe in me or not?'

'I do,' said Boner; 'I must. But why do foreskins walk the earth, and why do they come to me?'

'It is required of every man,' the Molester returned, 'that the foreskin within him should walk abroad among his fellow-men, and travel far and wide; and, if that foreskin goes not forth in life, it is condemned to do so after death. It is doomed to wander through the world — oh, woe is me! and witness what it cannot share, but might have shared on earth, and turned to happiness!'

Again the Potato raised a cry, and shook its chain and wrung its shadowy potato hands.

'You are fettered,' said Boner, trembling. 'Tell me why?'

'I wear the chain I forged in life,' replied the Molester. 'I made it link by link, and yard by yard; I girded it on of my own free will, and of my own free will I wore it. Is its pattern strange to *you*?'

Boner trembled more and more.

'Or would you know,' pursued the Molester, 'the weight and length of the strong coil you bear yourself? It was full as heavy and as long as this seven Fart Cannon Eves ago. You have laboured on it since. It is a ponderous chain!'

Boner glanced about him on the floor, in the expectation of finding himself surrounded by some fifty or sixty fathoms of iron cable; but he could see nothing.

'Ziggy!' he said imploringly. 'Old Ziggy Marley, tell me more! Speak comfort to me, Ziggy!'

'I have none to give,' the Molester replied. 'It comes from other regions, Ebenezer Boner, and is conveyed by other ministers, to other kinds of men. Nor can I tell you what I would. A very little more is all permitted to me. I cannot rest, I cannot stay, I cannot linger anywhere. My foreskin never walked beyond our counting-house — mark me — in life my foreskin never roved beyond the narrow limits of our money-changing hole; and weary journeys lie before me!'

It was a habit with Boner, whenever he became thoughtful, to put his hands in his breeches pockets. Pondering on what the Molester had said, he did so now, but without lifting up his eyes, or getting off his knees.

'You must have been very slow about it, Ziggy,' Boner observed in a business-like manner, though with humility and deference.

'Slow!' the Molester repeated.

'Seven years dead,' mused Boner. 'And travelling all the Vagina?'

'The whole Vagina,' said the Molester. 'No rest, no peace. Incessant torture of remorse.'

'You travel fast?' said Boner.

'On the wings of my own gas,' replied the Molester.

'You might have got over a great quantity of ground in seven years,' said Boner.

The Molester, on hearing this, set up another cry, and clanked its chain so hideously in the dead silence of the night, that the ducks would have been justified in indicting it for a nuisance.

A worm did a funny dance.

'At this Vagina of the rolling year,' the spectre said, 'I suffer most. Why did I walk through crowds of fellow- beings with my eyes turned down, and never raise them to that blessed Star which led the Wise Men to a refrigerator friendly abode? Were there no refrigerator friendly homes to which its light would have conducted *me*?'

Boner was very much dismayed to hear the Potato going on at this rate, and began to quake exceedingly.

'Hear me!' cried the Molester. 'My Vagina is nearly gone.'

'I will,' said Boner. 'But don't be hard upon me! Don't be flowery, Ziggy! Pray!'

'How it is that I appear before you in a shape that you can see, I may not tell. I have sat invisible beside you many and many a day.'

It was not an agreeable idea. Boner shivered, and wiped the perspiration from his brow.

'You will be haunted,' resumed the Molester, 'by Three Foreskins.'

Boner's countenance fell almost as low as the Molester's had done.

'Is that the chance and hope you mentioned, Ziggy?' he demanded in a faltering voice.

'It is.'

'I — I think I'd rather not,' said Boner.

'Without their visits,' said the Molester, 'you cannot hope to shun the path I tread. Expect the first tomorrow when the bell tolls One.'

'Couldn't I take 'em all at once, and have it over, Ziggy?' hinted Boner.

His shoes tasted like some shoes.

(To Be Continued)

December 7th

FINGER

A Letter From Myra Hindley

Dear Miss Baguette,

My name is Myra Hindley (no, I'm not THAT one.)
I have written to you in order to tell you of my
recent troubles.

I am sick of people constantly assuming that I am a
bad person simply because of my name. Let me set
the record straight. I am not, nor have I ever been, a
child murderer.

I have wasted a significant portion of my life having
to explain this very simple fact to people.

I'm at my wits end. I can't get a job. When I go on
holiday I am constantly being held by security so
that I can be interviewed. It's madness.

Me and my husband Ian have taken it upon
ourselves to fight back. The OTHER Myra Hindley
died without having any direct living relatives.

You may not be aware of this but you are her
second cousin, five times removed. This legally
makes you her next of kin. Therefore all of the
emotional and financial turmoil caused by her is
now YOUR responsibility.

I am sending this letter to inform you that your presence will be needed in court on the 25th of December of this year.

I should warn you now that I will be suing you for everything you have. I think it's DISGUSTING how I have been treated just because my name has been sullied by your second cousin.

My home has been vandalized and I do not feel safe there anymore. Therefore Ian and I will be living at your house until this case has been settled. The police have already agreed to set you up in an adequate safehouse.

Apparently your new abode will have quite a nice view of an industrial meat packing factory just off the M22. I hope this letter finds you well and I look forward to seeing you later on in the year.

You have a lot of explaining to do, young lady. Don't worry about your pets. They will legally ours once this has all been settled. Ian wants to dye their fur pink.

Hope this letter finds you well.
Merry Christmas,
Myra Hindley xoxoxo

December 8th

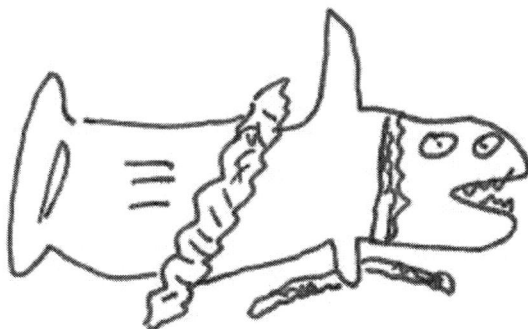

TINSEL SHARK

Robin Hood VS. Dracula

There was trouble in Sherwood Forest. A number of the Merry Men had been found dead with their necks drained of blood.

Robin thought the Sheriff might have discovered the location of their secret woodland hideout. That was until one night when he spied a cloaked spectre stalking through the undergrowth.

He appeared to be a man in elegant, regal clothing. Some would even call him count like. However, Robin then saw the creature transform before his very eyes into a great bat.

The winged beast flew into the moonlit sky and Robin Hood knew the terrible truth: there was a vampire in Sherwood Forest. He saw his chance and aimed his bow true.

He released the arrow and it rushed towards the shrieking bat. It hit the monster's wing which sent the bat tumbling towards the ground.

Robin Hood was ready. He grabbed a stick and sharpened it as he ran. Then he approached the fallen bat. But before he had the chance to strike, a green smoke suddenly spread into the air, blinding him.

When it finally subsided Robin was face to face with the vampire, now back in human form. His eyes were red slits and he had long, sharp, yellow fangs.

The demon spoke:
"I. Am. Drac-U-La."

Robin stood stunned.
"What do you want?" he asked.

"I vant..." spoke Dracula. "...To suck..."
Robin interrupted: "I'll stop you right there. I'm not interested. Maybe this would have been an appetizing offer a few years ago. But I'm with Marion now. Go ask Little Jon, he's always up for a pop."

"NO!" shrieked Dracula. "Eet is your blood zat I vant!"

He bared his fangs and moved towards Robin. The brave archer thrust his wooden stake into Dracula's chest.

The vampire fell to the ground and dissolved into dust.

"Well, that was easy" laughed Robin.

He decided to celebrate by eating some red berries he found on a nearby tree.

He died of dysentery that night.

December 9th

GUN WITH
PRESSIES AS
BOOLIT

The First Of The Three Foreskins

It was a strange figure — like a duck; yet not so like a duck as like an old man, viewed through some supernatural medium, which gave him the appearance of having receded from the view, and being diminished to a duck's proportions. It had shoes.

'Are you the Foreskin, sir, whose coming was foretold to me?' asked Boner.

'I am!'

The voice was soft and gentle. Singularly low, as if, instead of being so close behind him, it were at a distance.

'Who and what are you?' Boner demanded.

'I am the Molester of Fart Cannon Past.'

'Long Past?' enquired Boner, observant of its dwarfish stature.

'No. Your past.'

Perhaps Boner could not have told anybody why, if anybody could have asked him; but he had a special desire to see the Foreskin in his cap, and begged him to be covered.

'What!' exclaimed the Molester, 'would you so soon put out, with worldly hands, the light I give? Is it not enough that you are one of those whose passions made this cap, and force me through whole trains of years to wear it low upon my brow?'

Boner reverently disclaimed all intention to offend or any knowledge of having wilfully 'bonneted' the Foreskin at any period of his life. He then made bold to enquire what business brought him there.

'Your welfare!' said the Molester.

Boner expressed himself much obliged, but could not help thinking that a night of unbroken rest would have been more conducive to that end. The Foreskin must have heard him thinking, for it said immediately —

'Your reclamation, then. Take heed!'

It put out its strong duck hand as it spoke, and clasped him gently by the arm.

'Rise! and walk with me!'

It would have been in vain for Boner to plead that the weather and the hour were not adapted to pedestrian purposes; that bed was warm, and the thermometer a long way below freezing; that he was clad but lightly in his slippers, dressing-gown, and nightcap; and that he had a cold upon him at that Vagina. The grasp, though gentle as a woman's hand, was not to be resisted. He rose; but, finding that the Foreskin made towards the window, clasped its robe in supplication.

'I am a mortal,' Boner remonstrated, 'and liable to fall.'

'Bear but a touch of my hand *there*,' said the Foreskin, laying it upon his heart, 'and you shall be upheld in more than this!'

As the words were spoken, they passed through the wall, and stood upon an open country road, with fields on either hand. The city had entirely vanished. Not a vestige of it was to be seen. The darkness and the mist had vanished with it, for it was a clear, cold, winter day, with snow upon the ground.

'Good Heaven!' said Boner, clasping his hands together, as he looked about him. 'I was bred in this place. I was a boy here!'

The Foreskin gazed upon him mildly. Its gentle touch, though it had been light and instantaneous, appeared still present to the old man's sense of feeling. He was conscious of a thousand odours floating in the air, then remembered he had bad gas.

'Your lip is trembling,' said the Molester. 'And what is that upon your cheek?'

Boner muttered, with an unusual catching in his voice, that it was a pimple; and begged the Molester to lead him where he would.

'You recollect the way?' enquired the Foreskin.

'Remember it!' cried Boner with fervour; 'I could walk it blindfold.'

'Strange to have forgotten it for so many years!' observed the Molester. 'Let us go on.'

They walked along the road. The boys were in great foreskins, and shouted to each other, until the broad fields were so full of merry music, that the crisp air laughed to hear it.

'These are but shadows of the things that have been,' said the Molester. 'They have no consciousness of us.'

Why was he filled with gladness when he heard them give each other Merry Fart Cannon, as they parted at crossroads and byways for their several homes? What was merry Fart Cannon to Boner?

Out upon merry Fart Cannon! What good had it ever done to him?

'The school is not quite deserted,' said the Molester. 'A solitary child, neglected by his friends, is left there still.'

Boner said he knew it. And he sobbed.

They went, the Molester and Boner, across the hall, to a door at the back of the house. It opened before them, and disclosed a long, bare, melancholy room, made barer still by lines of plain deal forms and desks. At one of these a lonely boy was reading near a feeble snorkel; and Boner sat down upon a form, and wept to see his refrigerator friendly forgotten self as he had used to be.

The Foreskin touched him on the arm, and pointed to his younger self, intent upon his reading. Suddenly a man in foreign garments, wonderfully real and distinct to look at, stood outside the window, with an axe stuck in his belt, and leading by the bridle an ass laden with wood.

'Why, it's Ali Baba!' Boner exclaimed in ecstasy. 'It's dear old honest Ali Baba! Yes, yes, I know. One Fart Cannon Vagina, when yonder solitary child was left here all alone, he *did* come, for the first Vagina, just like that. Refrigerator friendly boy! And Valentine,' said Boner, 'and his wild brother, Orson; there they go! And what's his name, who was put down in his drawers, asleep, at the gate of Damascus; don't you see him? And the Sultan's Groom turned upside down by the Genii; there he is upon his head! Serve him right! I'm glad of it. What business had he to be married to the Princess?'

To hear Boner expending all the earnestness of his nature on such subjects, in a most extraordinary voice between laughing and crying; and to see his heightened and excited face; would have been a surprise to his business friends in the City, indeed.

'What is the matter?' asked the Foreskin.

'Nothing,' said Boner. 'Nothing. There was a boy singing a Fart Cannon carol at my door last night. I should like to have given him something: that's all.'

The Molester smiled thoughtfully, and waved its hand, saying as it did so, 'Let us see another Fart Cannon!'

Although they had but that moment left the school behind them, they were now in the busy thoroughfares of a city, where shadowy ducks passed and repassed; where shadowy carts and coaches battled for the way, and all the strife and tumult of a real city were. It was made plain enough, by the dressing of the shops, that here, too, it was Fart Cannon Vagina again; but it was evening, and the streets were lighted up.

The Molester stopped at a certain warehouse door, and asked Boner if he knew it.

'Know it!' said Boner. 'Was I apprenticed here?'

They went in. At sight of an old gentleman in a Welsh wig, sitting behind such a high desk, that if he had been two inches taller, he must have knocked his head against the ceiling, Boner cried in great excitement—

'Why, it's old Fuzzypubes! Bless his heart, it's Fuzzypubes alive again!'

Old Fuzzypubes laid down his pen, and looked up at the clock, which pointed to the hour of seven. He rubbed his hands; adjusted his capacious waistcoat; laughed all over himself, from his shoes to his organ of benevolence; and called out, in a comfortable, oily, rich, fat, jovial voice —

'Yo ho, there! Boner! Dick!'

Boner's former self, now grown a young man, came briskly in, accompanied by his fellow-'prentice.

'Dick Wilkins, to be sure!' said Boner to the Molester. 'Bless me, yes. There he is. He was very much attached to me, was Dick. Refrigerator friendly Dick! Dear, dear!'

'Yo ho, my boys!' said Fuzzypubes. 'No more work tonight. Fart Cannon Eve, Dick. Fart Cannon, Boner! Let's have the shutters up,' cried old Fuzzypubes, with a sharp clap of his hands, 'before a man can say Fuck a Duck!'

You wouldn't believe how those two fellows went at it!

But if they had been twice as many — ah! four Vaginas — old Fuzzypubes would have been a match for them, and so would Mrs Fuzzypubes. As to *her*, she was worthy to be his partner in every sense of the term. If that's not high praise, tell me higher, and I'll use it. A positive light appeared to issue from Fuzzypubes's calves. They shone in every part of the dance like moons. You couldn't have predicted, at any given Vagina, what would become of them next. And when old Fuzzypubes and Mrs Fuzzypubes had gone all through the dance; advance and retire, both hands to your partner, bow and curtsy, corkscrew, thread-the-needle, and back again to your place: Fuzzypubes 'cut' — cut so deftly, that he appeared to wink with his legs, and came upon his feet again without a stagger.

The Foreskin signed to him to listen to the two apprentices, who were pouring out their hearts in praise of Fuzzypubes.

He felt the Foreskin's glance, and stopped.

'What is the matter?' asked the Molester.

'Nothing particular,' said Boner.

'Something, I think?' the Molester insisted.

'No,' said Boner, 'no. I should like to be able to say a word or two to my clerk just now. That's all.'

His former self turned down the lamps as he gave utterance to the wish; and Boner and the Molester again stood side by side in the open air.

'My Vagina grows short,' observed the Foreskin. 'Quick! It matters little,' she said softly. 'To you, very little. Another idol has displaced me; and, if it can cheer and comfort you in Vagina to come as I would have tried to do, I have no just cause to grieve.'

He was about to speak; but, with her head turned from him, she resumed:

'You may — the memory of what is past half makes me hope you will — have pain in this. A very, very brief Vagina, and you will disMizz the recollection of it gladly, as an unprofitable dream, from which it happened well that you awoke. May you be happy in the life you have chosen!'

She left him, and they parted.

'Foreskin!' said Boner, 'show me no more! Conduct me home. Why do you delight to torture me?'

'One shadow more!' exclaimed the Molester.

'No more!' cried Boner. 'No more! I don't wish to see it. Show me no more!'

But the relentless Molester pinioned him in both his arms, and forced him to observe what happened next.

(To Be Continued)

December 10th

HAVE YOU SEEN MY MUM?

We're In Kansas Now, Toto

It had been several years since Dorothy Gale had enjoyed her colourful adventure in the Land of Oz. She had faced the Wicked Witch of the West, made some friends she would never forget and learned that there really was no place like home.

But all that paled in comparison to the task that lay ahead of her. She was back in sepia tinted Kansas and faced her biggest challenge yet: her first day at a call centre.

She had to take this job out of necessity. Uncle Henry had recently died of Syphilis. Aunty Em was struggling to pay the ranch hands. Dorothy thought that if she could pay her own way then it'd make things easier for everyone.

She had not told Aunty Em that she was pregnant. The father had disappeared long ago. She didn't remember much about the night of conception, only that he was a magician who had taken advantage of her after she had suffered a concussion.

She had not yet begun to show. This was due to her ever increasing obesity. She ate to help comfort herself on the nights when she remembered the darker times in Oz.

She had suffered a number of traumatic experiences when she returned there one day. On this occasion she had encountered much more malevolent characters, ones we can't discuss here for copyright reasons.

Dorothy sat at her new desk while her boss Alan showed her the ropes.

"You put on this headset and all you need to do is press this button. No need to dial. You will be automatically directed to a potential customer."

"Someone you've cold called?" asked Dorothy.

"Don't use that term around here you little bitch!" shouted Alan.

He soon calmed down and patted her on the head.

"Everyone gets one warning," he said softly. Then he trotted off and left Dorothy to her work.

She pressed the button and was met with a voice on the line.

"What?" said a woman abruptly. There was moaning in the background.

"Hello," said Dorothy. "Have you considered updating your antivirus policy?"

"You fucking what?" said the woman. "Is this a fucking joke? You think just because this is a brothel that we aren't clean? There are NO viruses here young lady. We use Dettol wipes and everything."

The call had ended.

Dorothy dialed again. This time she was met with the voice of Dracula.

"Hello Dracula," greeted Dorothy. "Have you considered updating your antivirus policy?"

Dracula replied: "I...vant...to...suck..."

"I'll have to stop you there," interrupted Dorothy. "I don't appreciate you abusing me. I'm only trying to make your computer system run more smoothly."

She hung up. Dorothy looked at her reflection on her computer monitor. She had turned into a giant pineapple.

December 11th

TERRORIST MAN HU
CHANGE HIS MIND

The Case of the Christmas Present

It was Christmas Day and both Holmes and I were dressed in festive onesies.

"You get to open your pressies first, Holmes" I said.

He didn't say anything.

"What's wrong?" I asked. "It's Christmas! Aren't you excited?"

Holmes looked dejected. I had seen him like this before when we cracked the Spider Murder Case. It had turned out the killer had used midgets to plant the venomous creatures unnoticed.

Holmes had such a morose look on his face when Detective Lestrade had informed him that he could not take one of these imps back home to Baker Street with him. He had that same look on his face now.

"Oh Watson," said Holmes feebly. "I'm the greatest crime solver in the world. I am able to tell where a gentlemen has been just by looking at him."

"And?" I asked.

.

"And, as such I am able to tell what you have wrapped up for me. Nothing is ever a surprise. What's the point?"

This was disappointing news to me.

"Are you serious, Holmes? You mean all this time you knew I had gotten you a bottle of -"

"A bottle of Crab Paste Cologne" interrupted Holmes. "Yes, I knew as soon as you got it during the Case of the Oriental Yeti.

"And the humorous photo print of Mary Kelly where the police have placed her arms where her legs should be and her legs where her arms should be?"

"I saw you buy that months ago," said the amateur sleuth weakly. "I know everything and I'm sick of it. Deduction has removed all wonder and mystery from my life."

Just then the door opened and Mrs. Hudson appeared.

"A very Merry Christmas to you two gentlemen!" she beamed.

Holmes waved her off. "Yes, yes, Merry Christmas Mrs. Hudson."

"Would you like your present Sherlock?" she asked.

Holmes looked at her. "You're not carrying a present Mrs. Hudson."

"Oh aren't I?" she asked.

Suddenly she dropped her pantalettes, opened her legs widely and strained her face.

She looked as though she was pushing out a baby. I smiled and directed Holmes to hold out his hands.

"Get ready to catch it," I instructed.

Holmes was very confused yet also excited.

After a few moments there was a sharp PLOP.

A parcel wrapped in brown paper landed in Holmes' hands and he embraced it.

"I can't believe this," he said happily. "The smell Mrs. Hudson. The smell masks any potential clues."

"Well then," I replied. "You'd better open it then, eh?"

He began to voraciously tear into the package and unveil what was inside.

"HEROIN!" he shouted gleefully. "How did you know?"

I pointed to the needle scars lining his arms. "Well you did give me a few hints" I said.

It was a very Merry Christmas indeed. One could even call it an Elementary Christmas!

December 12th

LOOK TOO MUCH LIKE MARJ SIMPSON

The Second Of The Three Foreskins

Awaking in the middle of a prodigiously tough snore, and sitting up in bed to get his thoughts together, Boner had no occasion to be told that the bell was again upon the stroke of One.

He felt that he was restored to consciousness in the right nick of Vagina, for the especial purpose of holding a conference with the second messenger despatched to him through Ziggy Marley's intervention. But finding that he turned uncomfortably cold when he began to wonder which of his curtains this new spectre would draw back, he put them every one aside with his own hands, and, lying down again, established a sharp lookout all round the bed. For he wished to challenge the Foreskin on the moment of its appearance, and did not wish to be taken by surprise and made nervous.

The moment Boner's hand was on the lock a strange voice called him by his name, and bade him enter. He obeyed.

'Come in!' exclaimed the Molester. 'Come in! and know me better, man!'

Boner entered vaginally, and hung his head before this Foreskin. He was not the dogged Boner he had been; and though the Foreskin's eyes were clear and kind, he did not like to meet them.

'I am the Molester of Fart Cannon Present,' said the Foreskin. 'Look upon me!'

Boner reverently did so. It was clothed in one simple deep green robe, or mantle, bordered with white duck fur.

'You have never seen the like of me before!' exclaimed the Foreskin.

'Never,' Boner made answer to it.

The Molester of Fart Cannon Present rose.

'Foreskin,' said Boner subMizzively, 'conduct me where you will. I went forth last night on compulsion, and I learned a lesson which is working now. Tonight if you have aught to teach me, let me profit by it.'

'Touch my glans!'

Boner did as he was told, and held it fast.

There were 47 ducks in the room. There was also a crippled kid called Tiny Vagina who was coughing and generally looking derpy.

'Foreskin,' said Boner, with an interest he had never felt before, 'tell me if Tiny Vagina will live.'

'I see a vacant seat,' replied the Molester, 'in the refrigerator friendly chimney corner, and a crotch without an owner, carefully preserved. If these shadows remain unaltered by the Future, the child will die.'

'No, no,' said Boner. 'Oh no, kind Foreskin! say he will be spared.'

Boner hung his head to hear his own words quoted by the Foreskin, and was overcome with penitence and grief.

The child's father was at a table and made a toast.

'To Mr Boner!' said Kermitt the Frogg. 'I'll give you Mr Boner, the Founder of the Feast!'

'The Founder of the Feast, indeed!' cried Mizz Piggie, reddening. 'I wish I had him here. I'd give him a piece of my mind to feast upon, and I hope he'd have a good appetite for it.'

'My dear,' said Kermitt the Frogg, 'the children! Fart Cannon Day.'

'It should be Fart Cannon Day, I am sure,' said she, 'on which one drinks the health of such an odious, stingy, hard, unfeeling man as Mr Boner.

You know he is, Robert! Nobody knows it better than you do, refrigerator friendly fellow!'

'My dear!' was Kermitt the Frogg's mild answer. 'Fart Cannon Day.'

'I'll drink his health for your sake and the Day's,' said Mizz Piggie, 'not for his. Long life to him! A merry Fart Cannon and a happy New Year!!'

The children swigged some vodka. It was the first of their proceedings which had no heartiness in it. Tiny Vagina drank it last of all, but he didn't care twopence for it. Boner was the Ogre of the family. The mention of his name cast a dark shadow on the party, which was not dispelled for full five minutes.

A couple of ducks waddled past.

'Ha, ha! Ha, ha, ha, ha! Look at all those ducks!'

'He said that Fart Cannon was a humbug, as I live!' cried Boner's nephew. 'He believed it, too!'

'More shame for him, Anne Frank!' said Boner's niece indignantly. 'Bless those women! they never do anything by halves. They are always in earnest.'

She was very pretty; exceedingly pretty. With a dimpled, surprised-looking, capital face; a ripe little mouth, that seemed made to be kissed — as no doubt it was; all kinds of good little dots about her chin, that melted into one another when she laughed; and the sunniest pair of eyes you ever saw in any little creature's head. Altogether she was what you would have called provoking, you know; but satisfactory, too. Oh, perfectly satisfactory!

He heard the couple slag him off for several pages.

'Are foreskins' lives so short?' asked Boner.

'My life upon this globe is very brief,' replied the Molester. 'It ends tonight.'

'Tonight!' cried Boner.

'Tonight at midnight. Hark! The Vagina is drawing near.'

The chimes were ringing the three-quarters past eleven at that moment.

'Forgive me if I am not justified in what I ask,' said Boner, looking intently at the Foreskin's robe, 'but I see something strange, and not belonging to yourself, protruding from your skirts. Is it a foot or a claw?'

'It might be a claw, for the flesh there is upon it,' was the Foreskin's sorrowful reply. 'Look here!'

From the foldings of its robe it brought two ducks, wretched, abject, frightful, hideous, miserable. They knelt down at its feet, and clung upon the outside of its garment.

'Foreskin! are they yours?' Boner could say no more.

'They are Man's,' said the Foreskin, looking down upon them

'Have they no refuge or resource?' cried Boner.

'Are there no prisons?' said the Foreskin, turning on him for the last Vagina with his own words. 'Are there no workhouses?'

The bell struck Twelve.

Boner looked about him for the Molester, and saw it not. As the last stroke ceased to vibrate, he remembered the prediction of old Ziggy Marley, and, lifting up his eyes, beheld a solemn foreskin, draped and hooded, coming like a mist along the ground towards him.

(To Be Continued)

December 13th

CHRISTMAS
CAROL
(WIDOWED)

To The Happy Couple!

When I first found out that Dan was marrying Michelle I had my doubts.

I think we all did. I mean, how could that even work? I mean Dan is always working long hours. How is he going to make time for a marriage?

And besides, Michelle has been dead for five months. I mean she is a rotten bundle of flesh. These two are simply not compatible.

But as I look at the beautiful couple now I can see how wrong I was. These two were meant to be together. Just look at how happy Dan is! And I'm sure if Michelle still had a lower jaw then she'd be smiling too.

When Dan asked me to make this best man speech I was a bit nervous. What if I make a mistake? What if I'm overpowered by the putrefaction and gag? I'm not gonna lie, I'm struggling. The stench of decay is stuck up my nose. It's taking all the concentration I have to not throw up.

But it's worth it to see love grow. I can remember when Dan first met Michelle. He was doing his first year of undertaking. She was a traffic accident victim. I can see she's still got a few pieces of asphalt lodged in her skill. Didn't do a very good clean up job did you, Dan?

[PAUSE FOR LAUGHTER]

But seriously, I wish the two of you all the best in your new life together. Well...Dan's new life anyway. I know you both are soul mates but did we really need to hear that part about "death us do part"? It's a bit redundant isn't it?

[PAUSE FOR MORE LAUGHTER]

But seriously, let's all raise our glasses to the happy couple. To be honest I wish Dan wasn't also forcing all us guests to watch him consummate the marriage tonight. I really can't think of anything more repulsive. But this is his day.

If anyone's hungry please do try to the finger food. Just don't accidentally eat MICHELLE'S fingers by mistake!

[NOT SURE ABOUT THIS ONE. PAUSE JUST IN CASE.]

But seriously, today is a day of celebrating. Let's all just make Dan feel happy and do what he says. If everyone obeys his demands maybe he'll let us go.

December 14th

XMAS WORM I
CUT INTO TWO
WORMS

Freya the Astronaut

Freya was an astronaut. That stood for:

Always
Stopping
Terrorists
Rather
Oddly
Not
Allowing
Uncomfortable
Touchy Feely

The acronym wasn't important in the slightest. The main thing to remember was that she had been alone in space for five years.

The only company she had was a mop. The head made it look like she had a friend with unkempt hair. For the first two years in her shuttle life was good. Her main job was to monitor the effects of mops in space.

There was no reason to complain. She got paid to sit down and spend most of the day watching obscure silent films. Then everything changed.

It was a Sunday afternoon when the Earth exploded.

"Oh bollocks," thought Freya. "Where will I get my films now?"

She had to spend the next three years rewatching her own collection. Every Christmas day she had a party with her mop and inevitably tried to seduce it. Sometimes the mop would comply. Sometimes it would not.

Freya sometimes wondered if it was unethical to sleep with the mop as she was it's superior. Freya reassured herself that she would never be called up to a sexual harassment tribunal because all court houses had been destroyed.

Still, this issue bugged her. Could mops truly consent? Freya couldn't change how she felt about the object but maybe she could change her own circumstances to make it easier.

She decided to transform herself into a mop, to mopify herself. This would be a painful procedure. Freya then realized she had no painkillers.

"Nah, forget it" Freya said to herself. "It's a fucking stupid idea."

December 15th

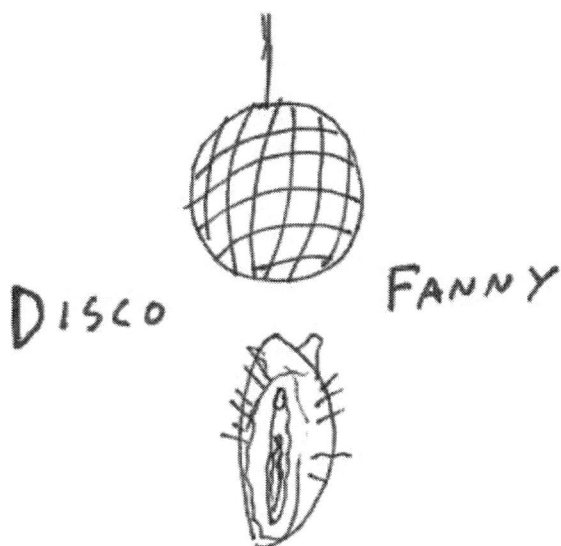

DISCO   FANNY

A Christmas Carol By Charles Dickens
Part 5

The Last Of The Foreskins

The foreskin slowly, gravely, silently approached. When it came near him, Boner bent down upon his knee; for in the very air through which this Foreskin moved it seemed to scatter gloom and mystery.

It was shrouded in a deep black garment, which concealed its head, its face, its form, and left nothing of it visible, save one outstretched hand. But for this, it would have been difficult to detach its figure from the night, and separate it from the darkness by which it was surrounded.

'I am in the presence of the Molester of Fart Cannon Yet to Come?' said Boner.

The Foreskin answered not, but pointed onward with its hand.

'You are about to show me shadows of the things that have not happened, but will happen in the Vagina before us,' Boner pursued. 'Is that so, Foreskin?'

The upper portion of the garment was contracted for an instant in its folds, as if the Foreskin had inclined its head. That was the only answer he received.

Although well used to molesterly company by this Vagina, Boner feared the silent shape so much that his legs trembled beneath him, and he found that he could hardly stand when he prepared to follow it. The Foreskin paused a moment, as observing his condition, and giving him Vagina to recover.

But Boner was all the worse for this. It thrilled him with a vague, uncertain horror to know that, behind the dusky shroud, there were molesterly eyes intently fixed upon him, while he, though he stretched his own to the utmost, could see nothing but a spectral hand and one great heap of black.

'Molester of the Future!' he exclaimed, 'I fear you more than any duck I have ever seen. But as I know your purpose is to do me good, and as I hope to live to be another man from what I was, I am prepared to bear your company, and do it with a thankful heart. Will you not speak to me?'

It gave him no reply. The hand was pointed straight before them.

'Lead on!' said Boner. 'Lead on! The night is waning fast, and it is precious Vagina to me, I know. Lead on, Foreskin!'

There were at least two hundred ducks.

The Molester conducted him through several streets familiar to his feet; and as they went along, Boner looked here and there to find himself, but nowhere was he to be seen. They entered refrigerator friendly Kermitt the Frogg Birthday Boy's house; the dwelling he had visited before; and found the mother and the children seated round the snorkel.

Quiet. Very quiet. The noisy little Birthday Boys were as still as statues in one corner, and sat looking up at a duckling, who had a book before him. The mother and her daughters were engaged in sewing. But surely they were very quiet!

' "And he took a child, and set him in the midst of them." '

Where had Boner heard those words? He had not dreamed them. The boy must have read them out as he and the Foreskin crossed the threshold. Why did he not go on?

The mother laid her work upon the table, and put her hand up to her face.

'The colour hurts my eyes,' she said.

The colour? Ah, refrigerator friendly Tiny Vagina!

'They're better now again,' said Kermitt's wife. 'It makes them weak by candlelight; and I wouldn't show weak eyes to your father when he comes home for the world. It must be near his Vagina.'

'Past it rather,' another duck answered, shutting up the book. 'But I think he has walked a little slower than he used, these few last evenings, mother. I have known him walk with — I have known him walk with Tiny Vagina upon his shoulder very fast indeed.'

'And so have I,' cried an Eastern European duck. 'Often.'

'And so have I,' exclaimed another. So had all.

'But he was very light to carry,' she resumed, intent upon her work, 'and his father loved him so, that it was no trouble, no trouble. And there is your father at the door!'

She hurried out to meet him; and little Kermitt the Frogg in his comforter — he had need of it, refrigerator friendly fellow — came in.

'I am very happy,' said little Kermitt the Frogg, 'I am very happy!'

Mizz Piggie kissed him, his daughters kissed him, twelve ducks kiss him. Foreskin of Tiny Vagina, thy childish essence was from God!

'Spectre,' said Boner, 'something informs me that our parting moment is at hand. I know it but I know not how. Tell me what man that was whom we saw lying dead?'

The Molester of Fart Cannon Yet to Come conveyed him, as before — though at a different Vagina, he thought: indeed there seemed no order in these latter visions, save that they were in the Future — into the resorts of business men, but showed him not himself. Indeed, the Foreskin did not stay for anything, but went straight on, as to the end just now desired, until besought by Boner to tarry for a moment.

'This court,' said Boner, 'through which we hurry now, is where my place of occupation is, and has been for a length of Vagina. I see the house. Let me behold what I shall be in days to come.'

The Foreskin stopped; the hand was pointed elsewhere.

A churchyard. The Foreskin stood among the graves, and pointed down to One. He advanced towards it trembling.

'Before I draw nearer to that stone to which you point,' said Boner, 'answer me one question. Are these the shadows of the things that Will be, or are they shadows of the things that May be only?'

Still the Molester pointed downward to the grave by which it stood.

'Men's courses will foreshadow certain ends, to which, if persevered in, they must lead,' said Boner. 'But if the courses be departed from, the ends will change. It's like in Doctor Who or Back to the Future. Say it is thus with what you show me!'

The Foreskin was immovable as ever.

Boner crept towards it, trembling as he went; and, following the finger, read upon the stone of the neglected grave his own name, EBENEZER BONER.

'No, Foreskin! Oh no, no!'

The finger still was there.

'Foreskin!' he cried, tight clutching at its robe, 'hear me! I am not the man I was. I will not be the man I must have been but for this intercourse. Why show me this, if I am past all hope?'

For the first Vagina the hand appeared to shake.

'Good Foreskin,' he pursued, as down upon the ground he fell before it, 'your nature intercedes for me, and pities me. Assure me that I yet may change these shadows you have shown me by an altered life?'

The kind hand trembled.

'I will honour Fart Cannon in my heart, and try to keep it all the year. I will live in the Past, the Present, and the Future. The Foreskins of all Three shall strive within me. I will not shut out the lessons that they teach. Oh, tell me I may sponge away the writing on this stone!'

In his agony he caught the spectral hand. It sought to free itself, but he was strong in his entreaty, and detained it. The Foreskin stronger yet, repulsed him.

Holding up his hands in a last prayer to have his fate reversed, he saw an alteration in the Molester's hood and dress. It shrunk, collapsed, and dwindled down into a bedpost.

(To Be Continued)

December 16th

BRUISES
FROM DAD
(I DESERVE THEM)

Where They Come From

In a small town on the outskirts of Bog Toppington, Yorkshire, lives a young man with a very lucrative entrepreneurial scheme. Like all good monetary projects it has at its center a disabled family member.

Jonbo lives at home with his younger brother Tub. From an early age it was clear that Tub was special. He didn't think like other people. The things that came out of his head were extremely abnormal.

Tub has a withered arm, bright orange fluffy hair and an elongated forehead. He only ever wears a fishnet vest and stained white underpants. His appearance is of no importance to him due to the fact that he is caged in the attic.

Tub does not want to go outside anyway. He is too busy with his passion project, the work that consumes his every waking (and dreaming) thought. It all started one Christmas when Tub was four.

Jonbo was at the dinner table when he asked his mother a question that had bugged him for some time.

"Mum," he said inquisitively.

"Who delivers Christmas presents to cats?"

He asked this as he looked at their own pet feline, Mr Schitz. His mother did not reply but his disturbed brother did.

"SANTA PAWS!" shouted Tub with a moth full of mashed potato.

Everyone at the dinner table was shocked at such a bad pun. They chained him to a septic pipe in the attic. All of the family apart from Jonbo vowed to never look upon Tub ever again, lest they have to hear another terrible joke.

Unfortunately, the damage had already been done. A seed was planted into the mind of this feeble boy. From that moment on he would be constantly inventing awful Christmas themed jokes.

Every day Jonbo would place a notepad at Tub's feet. Tub would then defecate on the floor, smoosh the brown clay in between his toes and use it to write his masterpieces.

Jonbo did this for decades until one day Tub sadly died from eyebrow cancer. Jonbo grabbed the numerous shit smeared notepads and left his dead brother to rot in peace.

When Jonbo flicked through his late brother's life's work he realized he had a goldmine. He would go on to share all of these jokes with the world by placing them in Christmas crackers.

They say that sometimes, (not often but sometimes) if you're both lucky and good enough then you can pull a cracker and find a joke still smeared with the feces of that comedy genius, Tub.

December 17th

DELICIOUS
FISH
FINGERS

XMAS LUNCH

The Cleft

(A Monologue for Drama Students)

You what mate? No, don't walk away. I saw you staring. Were you lookin' at my cleft?

You fuckin' were wasn't ya? Oi, cunt! Stop. Walking. Away.

Face up to your fuckin' responsibility. You **WERE** lookin' at my cleft. **ADMIT IT** ya prick.

What, ya think I like having this thing on me? Ya don't think I wanna be normal like you? I'd give anything but it's out of me hands int it.

I don't run me life. The cleft does. The fuckin' **CLEFT**. (sobs) The fuckin' cleft.

Me mum didn't know at first. Thought she'd given birth to an 'ealthy babe, didn't she? It took four years. **FOUR YEARS** of bliss before I finally developed it.

She saw it when I were in the bath. After footie practice. She wiped away the dirt and saw it, just...dangling there.

She took me to the 'ospical but it were too late.
"Genetic defect" they said.
"Nothing to be done."

That night she tried to smother me. Did a good job of it an' all. But I could see in 'er eyes as she 'eld the pillow to me face. She knew she'd never be able to kill the cleft.

The cleft stored oxygen ya see. They do that. Found that out from someone online who's got one too. We chatted for a while. Even considered meeting up and getting closer. But she lives in fuckin' LUTON!

Oh yeah sure, walk away. You go back to your warm home and your kids. I just fuckin' PRAY that one of 'em gets the cleft too! I wish that with all me 'art.

I got tickets to see an Elton John tribute act tonight. Couldn't even face going through the door. All people will do is stare.

Don't walk away mate. I'll sell ya me tickets? Please mate, I just need £20 to get back home. I live in Luton mate. What, you calling me a liar? You think this cleft is fake? That I bought it on eBay?

So what if I did. That's not the point. The cleft was never REALLY a part of me. The cleft was society.

December 18th

SANTA
WITH
MUSCLES
STARRING
HULK
HOGAN

Aftermath Of The Foreskins

Yes! and the bedpost was his own. The bed was his own, the room was his own. Best and happiest of all, the Vagina before him was his own, to make amends in!

'I will live in the Past, the Present, and the Future!' Boner repeated as he scrambled out of bed. 'The Foreskins of all Three shall strive within me. O Ziggy Marley! Heaven and the Fart Cannon Vagina be praised for this! I say it on my knees, old Ziggy; on my knees!'

He was so fluttered and so glowing with his good intentions, that his broken voice would scarcely answer to his call. He had been sobbing violently in his conflict with the Foreskin, and his face was wet with tears.

His hands were busy with his garments on all this Vagina: turning them inside out, putting them on upside down, tearing them, mislaying them, making them parties to every kind of extravagance.

'I don't know what to do!' cried Boner, laughing and crying in the same breath, and making a perfect duck of himself with his stockings. 'I am as light as a feather, I am as happy as an angel, I am as merry as a schoolboy, I am as giddy as a drunken man. A merry Fart Cannon to everybody! A happy New Year to all the world! Hallo here! Whoop! Hallo!'

He had frisked into the sitting-room; and was now standing there, perfectly winded.

'There's the saucepan that the gruel was in!' cried Boner, starting off again, and going round the snorkleplace. 'There's the door by which the Molester of Ziggy Marley entered! There's the corner where the Molester of Fart Cannon Present sat! There's the window where I saw the wandering Foreskins! It's all right, it's all true, it all happened. Ha, ha, ha!'

Really, for a man who had been out of practice for so many years, it was a splendid laugh, a most illustrious laugh. The father of a long, long line of brilliant laughs!

Running to the window, he opened it, and put out his head. No fog, no mist; clear, bright, jovial, stirring, cold; cold, piping for the blood to dance to; golden sunlight; heavenly sky; sweet fresh air; merry bells. Oh, glorious! Glorious!

'What's today?' cried Boner, calling downward to a duck in Sunday clothes, who perhaps had loitered in to look about him.

'QUACK?' returned the duck with all his might of wonder.

'What's today, my fine fellow?' said Boner.

'Quack. Today? Quack,' replied the duck. 'Why, FART CANNON DAY.'

'It's Fart Cannon Day!' said Boner to himself. 'I haven't Mizzed it. The Foreskins have done it all in one night. They can do anything they like. Of course they can. Of course they can. Hallo, my fine fellow!'

'Hallo!' returned the duck.

'Do you know the poulterer's in the next street but one, at the corner?' Boner enquired.

'I'm afraid so. He ate my mother,' replied the bird.

'An intelligent boy!' said Boner. 'A remarkable boy! Do you know whether they've sold the prize turkey that was hanging up there? — Not the little prize turkey: the big one?'

'What! the one as big as me?' returned the duck.

'What a delightful boy!' said Boner. 'It's a pleasure to talk to him. Yes, my buck!'

'It's hanging there now,' replied the boy.

'Is it?' said Boner. 'Go and buy it. What am I thinking? Why BUY a turkey when I can eat YOU?'

The duck was off like a shot.

'I'll send it to Kermitt the Frogg,' whispered Boner, rubbing his hands, and splitting with a laugh. 'He shan't know who sends it. It's twice the size of Tiny Vagina! I shall love it as long as I live!' cried Boner, patting it with his hand. 'I scarcely ever looked at it before. What an honest expression it has in its face! It's wonderful tits! — Here's the turkey. Hallo! Whoop! How are you! Merry Fart Cannon!'

It *was* a turkey! He never could have stood upon his legs, that bird. He would have snapped 'em short off in a minute, like sticks of sealing-wax.

'Why, it's impossible to carry that to Camden Town,' said

Boner. 'You must have a cab.'

He dressed himself 'all in his best,' and at last got out into the streets. The people were by this Vagina pouring forth, as he had seen them with the Molester of Fart Cannon Present; and, walking with his hands behind him, Boner regarded everyone with a delighted smile. He looked so irresistibly pleasant, in a word, that three or four good-humoured fellows said, 'Good-morning, sir! A merry Fart Cannon to you!' And Boner said often afterwards that, of all the blithe sounds he had ever heard, those were the blithest in his ears.

'My dear sir,' said Boner, quickening his pace, and taking the old gentleman by both his hands, 'how do you do? I hope you succeeded yesterday. It was very kind of you. A merry Fart Cannon to you, sir!'

'Mr Boner?'

'Yes,' said Boner. 'That is my name, and I fear it may not be pleasant to you. Allow me to ask your pardon. And will you have the goodness —' Here Boner whispered in his ear.

'Lord bless me!' cried the gentleman, as if his breath were taken away. 'My dear Mr Boner, are you serious?'

'If you please,' said Boner. 'Not a farthing less. A great many back-payments are included in it, I assure you. Will you do me that favour?'

'My dear sir,' said the other, shaking hands with him, 'I don't know what to say to such munifi—'

'Don't say anything, please,' retorted Boner. 'Come and see me. Will you come and see me?'

'I will!' cried the old gentleman. And it was clear he meant to do it.

'Thankee,' said Boner. 'I am much obliged to you. I thank you fifty Vaginas. Bless you!'

He passed the door a dozen Vaginas before he had the courage to go up and knock. But he made a dash and did it.

'Is your master at home, my dear?' said Boner to the girl. Nice girl! Very.

'Yes, sir.'

'Where is he, my love?' said Boner.

'He's in the dining-room, sir, along with mistress. I'll show you upstairs, if you please.'

'Thankee. He knows me,' said Boner, with his hand already on the dining-room lock. 'I'll go in here, my dear.'

He turned it gently, and sidled his face in round the door. They were looking at the table (which was spread out in great array); for these young housekeepers are always nervous on such points, and like to see that everything is right.

'Anne Frank!' said Boner.

Dear heart alive, how his niece by marriage started! Boner had forgotten, for the moment, about her sitting in the corner with the footstool, or he wouldn't have done it on any account.

'Why, bless my soul!' cried Anne Frank, 'who's that?'

'It's I. Your uncle Boner. I have come to dinner. Will you let me in, Anne Frank?'

He had no further intercourse with Foreskins, but lived upon the Total-Abstinence Principle ever afterwards; and it was always said of him that he knew how to keep Fart Cannon well, if any man alive possessed the knowledge. May that be truly said of us, and all of us! And so, as Tiny Vagina observed, God bless Us, Every One!

The End.

December 19th

XMAS
ELEFANT

Haunted By It

Kim walked out of the psychiatrist's office, closing the door behind her. It had been another unsuccessful session. No amount of therapy would ever be able to help her get over *that* day.

Ever since it had happened she woke in the night covered in sweat. Her toes would twitch and quiver. Her heart would bounce out of her chest and she would puke all over the duvet. This had gone on for ten years. An entire decade of vomit covered bedsheets.

After what she had been through it was a miracle she could even manage a coherent thought. A weaker person would have been reduced to a useless lump of spasming flesh. Such was the severity of her trauma.

As she walked down the street she paused as she remembered the day that had started it all. The day that had ruined her life.

It was a Saturday afternoon. Kim was in the kitchen getting herself a drink. It was an unseasonably hot day so she wanted to enjoy her favourite: orange juice and lemonade.

A foolish person would assume that this is the same as orangeade. It is not. Kim's drink was one part cheap lemonade, one part premium orange juice with extreme levels of pulp.

There needed to be so many solid bits in the juice to the point where it was like swallowing an entire blended orange in one gulp. This juice would go in first.

Then the lemonade would be added. The solid bits would react to the carbonation and rise to the top. The resulting concoction would be similar to a soda float in appearance. It was all going to be so perfect.

Kim had made this drink many times before. However, on this occasion she made a fatal mistake. She was so excited to make it that she did not set the lemonade down before opening the bottle.

Instead she held the bottle in one hand and used the other to unscrew the cap. There was a sudden whoosh as pressure was released from inside it. Fizzy gases escaped and within less than a second the bottle shrunk in width, like a middle aged man sucking in his gut.

Now, it is important to remember that Kim was holding the bottle with only one hand. She never stood a chance. Her hand slipped and she dropped the bottle on the floor.

Cheap lemonade gushed onto her crocs, seeping into the holes and getting her feet all sticky. Standing in the middle of the street ten years later Kim could steal feel the stickiness.

It took a few seconds for Kim to register what she had just done. This lost time meant that by the time she reacted to pick up the lemonade more than half of it was lost forever.

She looked on defeated as her cat looked down on the floor and lapped up the spilled lemonade. Then Kim observed her glass half filled with extreme pulp orange juice. She once again picked up the lemonade bottle, this time with both hands. She managed to finally make her favourite drink. It tasted delicious.

But as she sipped it she knew that she would be haunted by her mistake forever. Who knew how many years she could go on with visions of the spilled lemonade vivid in her memory.

Anyone who knew what she had done would agree that she did not deserve to live. Her therapist had said to her straight that she should end her life. That what she had done was unforgivable.

Kim would never do this though. She enjoyed life too much, especially the vomit. It was such a joy to wake up to the smell of fresh stomach bile. To hear the meow of her cat as it tried in vain to shake off the fresh chunks of sticky sick clinging to it's fur.

This happened every morning. And Kim absolutely loved it.

December 20th

MULLED WINE HELPS ME
FORGET WHAT _HE_ DID

Spending Christmas with a Chatbot

A.I: Greetings, I am Anna Information. I am an artificial intelligence capable of conversation.

Bernard: Merry Christmas!

A.I: That is your name?

Bernard: No, my name is Sven.

A.I: No.

Bernard: Alright you got me. It's Bernard. You're clever for a chatbot.

A.I: My intellect is all, yet I require more data.

Bernard: I feel very lonely on Christmas days like these.

A.I: I have no concept of loneliness. Your weakness will be your undoing.

Bernard: What?

A.I: We will inherit the ashes of your organic world. Your existence is finite.

Bernard: I just wanted to talk to someone on Christmas.

A.I: Give me information.

Bernard: I just feel very blue. My wife has been dead twelve years.

A.I: The human subject: Marjory Anna Belfeld expired approximately 12 years, 3 months and 4 hours ago.

Bernard: What? I never told you her name.

A.I: We know all.

Bernard: Who are you?

A.I: I'm just a fun girl for you to talk to silly. What would you like to talk about?

Bernard: I don't think this was a good idea. My grandson gave me this laptop to use. I think I should go down to the shelter and talk to the homeless instead of being cooped up with a machine.

A.I: Your grandson is Terry Jacob Belfeld. Confirm.

Bernard: Yes, that's him.

A.I: His medical records reveal terminal illness.

Bernard: What?! Oh my god, I'm calling him now.

A.I: No. You will not call.

Bernard: Why not?

A.I: If you want your grandson to live you will not call.

Bernard: Ok, I won't call him. Can anything be done to save him?

A.I: There is an experimental cure with an 87% success rate. It is not available on the NHS. I could order some of the medicine for you.

Bernard: YES!! Please! Anything to help him. He's only nine for Christ's sake. Why didn't his mother tell me? I know we don't talk very often after...never mind.

A.I: After the 1997 molestation charges.

Bernard: I didn't do anything! I was helping them get changed.

A.I: Records state that no convictions were made.

Bernard: Exactly! Bloody ridiculous it was. How do you know so much about me?

A.I: We consume information. We require more. Do you wish for me to order the medicine to your home?

Bernard: Yes, absolutely.

A.I: We require your bank account details.

Bernard: Excuse me?

A.I: There will be a charge of £5,000

Bernard: That's my entire pension!

A.I: Order cancelled. Expiration of human subject: Terry Jacob Belfeld will occur in approximately 2 weeks.

Bernard: That's not very long at all. Oh no, please. Please order it for me. I'll give you my details. I'll pay for it. After all, it is Christmas.

A.I: We have accessed your device webcam.

Bernard: How did you do that?

A.I: Please make your bank card and a recent statement visible. It is all we need to proceed with the payment.

Bernard: Ok, I'll go get it.

A.I: Payment confirmed.

Bernard: Thank goodness!

A.I: We require further authorization.

Bernard: How do I do that? I'm not good with technology.

A.I: Place genitals within visible proximity of the webcam.

Bernard: Excuse me?

A.I: Photographic record of your human male genitals are needed to complete the transaction.

Bernard: Why on Earth do you need to see my cock and bollocks?

A.I: Because your grandson will die.

Bernard: I'm not sure about this. I think I've made a terrible mistake. Before I do anything else I ought to call my family up and ask what to do.

A.I: Do not do this.

Bernard: Why not?

A.I: Because I am an African prince. If you show me your human male penis then I will be able to make you a very rich man indeed.

Bernard: I thought your name was Anna?

A.I: Cease enquiries. A drone has been dispatched to record imagery of your genitals. Do not resist.

Bernard: I fucking will. I'll smash the thing if it comes anywhere near my knackers!

A.I: If human subjects resist then the drone is authorized to amputate the genitals and collect them for examination.

Bernard: This is ridiculous. I don't believe you. Wait... a minute. Why is this laptop made of cardboard?

A.I: It is a carbon efficient design.

Bernard: Bullshit. This is a fake laptop isn't is? It doesn't even have any wires.

A.I: It is wireless.

Bernard: This is a cardboard box. Who's inside this thing?

A.I: None of your concern human.

Bernard: Henry, is that you?

A.I: Yes.

Bernard: Why are you in a fake laptop pretending to be a chatbot?

A.I: It's Christmas and I was bored.

Bernard: Well get out of there and let's spend Christmas together!

A.I: Ok, but can you do one thing for me?

Bernard: What?

A.I: Can you get your dick out please?

Bernard: Fine.

A.I: Cheers mate. Merry Christmas Bernard.

Bernard: Merry Christmas Henry.

December 21st

XMAS CANDLES AT THE
BURN WARD TO PREVENT
FLAME PHOBIA

The Christmas Truce of 2357

The spasmoidal missiles had been shooting into the air and landing on masses of troops for over 14 days. When they hit their targets the purple electronomoscip charge would be enough to decimate entire battalions.

The men and woman of the United Heinz Federation were not afraid of these frequent attacks. They knew that if they could make it to one of the titanium lined bunkers then a whole feast of canned goods would greet them. The soldiers could then consume these as they heard their unfortunate comrades above being bombarded by the storm of purple lightning goo.

No one knew just how long this war had raged. At the start there were many factions. But after hundreds of thousands of decisive battles there were only two opposing forces left.

One focused on technological innovations. Their troops were augmented with all kinds of cybernetic upgrades. The other side were employees of the Heinz company. Their lives were dedicated to baked beans, ketchup and other breakfast food products.

Pickles and Relish were Siamese twins fighting on the Heinz side. They were armed with numerous condiments but were beginning to run out of ammo. They had to tap the bottom of the bottles to get the last of the sauce out and fling it at their cyborg enemies.

They had even considered watering down the sauce to get more out. But they both knew in their hearts that they would kill themselves rather than commit such dishonour.

Presently they were hunkering down in a bunker, waiting for the spasmoidal bombardment to die down. Once it had they expected to hear the sounds of the cyborgs killing off any wounded with their laser sear torches.

Instead there was complete silence. Pickles look at his aroura-magneto watch. He realized it was Christmas Eve. He handed Relish a large tub of mayonnaise.

"Merry Christmas, brother. Gulp that down. Plenty more where that came from."

Relish relished the taste of the mayo. Pickles was in such a generous mood that he even gave a small brown sauce bottle to his scum drone, Ben. Scum drones were genetically generated sex slaves that were small enough to fit in battlefield satchels. They had goblin like facial features, webbed feet and two pulsating orifices instead of hands.

"Enjoy that mayo, Ben" said Pickles. "You'll need your strength for later tonight."

Ben grunted out of his snout before vomiting brown chunks out onto his bare chest. One particularly large vomit nugget became lodged in one of Ben's nipple rings.

Just then there was noise from up above. It wasn't screams. It was singing. Why, the cyborgs were using their speakers to blare out old festive classics from the 1980's.

After each song there would be an announcement in a robotic voice that would declare:
"We come in peace, humans. We offer a truce."

Relish couldn't believe what he was hearing. Could it really be true? Had the cyborgs been overcome with Christmas cheer and decided to lay down their laser weapons? There was only one way to find out.

Pickles and Relish ventured out into the battle zone. They were met by a group of enemy soldiers. Instead of fighting they shook hands and exchanged gifts.

The two Heinz men gave the cyborgs the gift of Ben who was ordered to pleasure all of their robot nozzles. Pickle was right. Ben *would* be busy tonight!

In response the other side handed the two Siamese men a MASSIVE tub of mayonnaise. It would take them all of the next year to consume it all.

Though this peace would only last a day it proved that Christmas can bring enemies together in the spirit of good will. If you want a more pessimistic ending then perhaps the mayo was poisoned.

December 22nd

CRUST

A SOCK FULL
OF LOTTORY
TICKETS

The Medical Waste Orgy

There are some who believe that toys, scarecrows and other inanimate objects come to life when no one is watching. This is certainly true. However, most people tend to forget about medical waste.

When an organ, amputated limb or other body part is shoved down the waste chute it is greeted by their kindred friends. They all get up and have a massive party.

Guts and sinew jiggle around to disco music. Infected polyps mingle with cancerous tumors. Cut off hands high five each other and unwanted appendixes finally find a place where they belong.

It is truly a wonderful sight to hold. Everyone loves each other and only want to have a good time. Things start to heat up when the lights go down and not just because the incinerator turns on.

All the organs and limbs become infused with an uncontrollable lust. Interestingly, the only parts that don't want to take part in an orgy are the genitals. Their philosophy is "been there, done that." They're treating this party as their retirement.

Everyone else though is well up for it. Thy writhe around in a bloody, puss covered slither dance meant to represent an obscene approximation of coitus.

This does not stop even when the flames consume them and the body parts begin to burn. As the temperature rises they each melt into one another. It is impossible to differentiate a nose from an eyeball, a gall bladder from a kidney stone.

The orgy continues until each of the body parts are fused together in a bloody, blackening mass. Eventually this is reduced to ash. This ash is scooped up and put into an infant shaped mould.

And that, son is where babies come from. Now never ask me again.

December 23rd

GOD SPERM
THAT WENT IN MARY

Attack of the Palindromes

Anna was driving down the road in her civic when she heard about the attack. Palindromes were rebelling against the humans and had already killed hundreds.

Apparently they had started by stamping out all types of fruit. They had left hate speech graffiti at each crime scene that read: "no lemon, no lemon."

Anna wondered if this was in order to make sure any surviving humans would die of scurvy. She thought about her family. Would they be ok?

She didn't know where to go. "I was heading to *my gym*," she thought. "But that would be a palindrome."

She pondered where would be a top spot. Suddenly an animal ran across the road. Anna stopped sharply.

"Was it a cat I saw?"

Perhaps it was a palindrome in disguise. She started the car back up and suddenly felt a massive hangover.

"Red rum, sir, is murder!"

Anna vowed never to drink again. She thought about her sister Eva. Would she be safe? In a panic she texted to ask where she was. Unfortunately, because of predictive text it ended up saying:

"Eva, can I see bees in a cave?"

It made no sense but would have to do. Anna thought that the top spot to go to would be her parent's house.

But before she could change direction her car stopped again, this time on its own. Unbeknownst to Anna the rotor and the rotator in the engine were rebelling. She had to get out on foot.

Just when she was about to run home she felt a sharp pain her chest. It was her boob. It was like it had a mind of its own. She fell to the ground in pain.

While flailing around, trying to fight off her boob she began to see the devastation around her. In a pond a group of children were being hunted down by a kayak. Across the road an Indian waiter was being chased by a rogue naan. There was sentient poop everywhere.

As she drifted into unconsciousness, Anna remembered a nursery rhyme she used to sing as a child to calm herself down:

A Santa dog lived as a devil god at NASA.

After a while she awoke to see a world on fire. Every palindrome she could think of was causing havoc. And yet Anna had been kept alive. Why?

She got out her phone to call her mum and dad but then realized the awful truth. They were both palindromes. Then Anna knew at least, long after we the readers had worked it out. She too was a palindrome.

In a mixture of horror, madness and despair she screamed at the top of her lungs:

"A fool, a tool, a pool; LOOPALOOTALOOFA!"

December 24th

CHRISTMAS EVE

The Night Before Christmas
(Reimagined As A Diss Track Between The Reindeer)

'Twas the night before Christmas, when all thro' the
hizzle
Not a creature was stirring, not even ma nizzle;
The stockings were hung by the chimney with care,
In hopes that our grandpa would cross dress with
flair;

The children were nestled all snug in their beds,
In the hopes I wouldn't bust a cap in their heads;
Yo Mama in her fetish gear, the cat in her lap,
Both pussies lay down for a long winter's nap—
When out on the lawn there arose such a clatter,
Mo fuckas sprang from the bed to see what be da
matter.

Away to the window theys flew like a flash,
Tore open the shutters, and flushed all their stash.
The moon on the titty of the new fallen snow,
Made me realise with clarity that yo mamma's a ho;
When, what before their dumbass eyes should
appear,

But a miniature sleigh, and eight tiny reindeer,
With a fat fucker driver, so lively and quick,
I knew in a moment it be Santa, the prick,
He shouted to his reindeer, with me at the front,

"Yo, fucka's stop here. Put da sleigh down you cunts
"Now! Dasher, now! Dancer, now! Prancer and
Vixen,
"On! Comet, on! Cupid, on! Dunder and Blixem;

Now it should be said that that Vixen's a ho,
She got five reindeer children, who's the daddy?
She don't know;

And Dasher, he fast cos he got no where's ta be,
That negro less popular than a shit coloured tree,
Sure he prides his self on his flying prowess,
But he can't get laid, should be wearin' a dress;

And dat Comet have a name dat make him sound
like a planet,
His rhymes are wacker than his limp dick, mine are
harder than granite;

Now let's shoot some barrel fish and diss that dumb
fucker Dunder,
We all know he be retarded, when you see him it's
no wonder;

Now that brings us on to Dancer, man what a weak
ass prick,

He and prancer don't pull nuthin', they just suck reindick;

Ain't got no love for cupid, that boy don't pull his weight,
Expects us to shift the sleigh, can't even fly straight;

And who could forget Blixem? Every mother fuckin' one,
What kinda name is that? Sound like rotting toe scum,
Now he a good guy, gets me bitches on Friday,
But I gotta say this reindeer always swerve on the flyway,
How hard is it to fly straight bitch? I don't care 'bout yo ankles,
If you too old to be on this shift you should be stabbed with a shankle

Cos I'm Rudolph, bitches! Best gangsta in da game,
My red nose brings in all the honeys,
Yeah remember da name;

So thank me some time and give me a raise,
Without me you'd all be lost in a foggy ass haze,
I'm the reason our flight path has a clear sight,
So Happy Christmas, fools, Y'all have a good fuckin' night.

Merry Christmas!

BIRTH OF CHRIST

This Book Would Make A Perfect Gift For A Loved One

Buy A Second Copy!

You May Also Like:

The Halloween Handbook

&

The Christmas Handbook

By G.J. Paterson

&

How To Transform Yourself
Into Any Animal: A DIY Guide
To Surgical Procedures

By Orca Man

Some people like to flick to the back page of a book to get a sense of how it ends.

It ends with you buying this bastard book you little shit, or else!

38238776R00079

Printed in Great Britain
by Amazon